*Last born, only poet — for Juliet,
who likes walking in the rain*

E. de R.

For Mum

B. L.

Text copyright © 2010 by Elena de Roo
Illustrations copyright © 2010 by Brian Lovelock

First U.S. edition 2011

Library of Congress Cataloging-in-Publication Data
is available.

Library of Congress Catalog Card Number pending

ISBN 978-0-7636-5313-2

LEO 15 14 13 12 11 10
10 9 8 7 6 5 4 3 2 1

Printed in Heshan, Guangdong, China

This book was typeset in Univers.
The illustrations were done in watercolor and ink.

Candlewick Press
99 Dover Street
Somerville, Massachusetts 02144

visit us at www.candlewick.com

THE RAIN TRAIN

ELENA DE ROO & BRIAN LOVELOCK

CANDLEWICK PRESS

When the rain fingers drum out a dance on the pane,
When the windows are foggy enough for my name,

A pitter-pat-pat, a pitter-pat-pat,
A pittery-pittery-pittery-pat.

When it's thundering down on the roof, in the lane,
From the storm comes the call . . .

"All aboard the Rain Train!"

Glide from the platform—

Tisssssshhhhhhhhhhhh.

Slow through the station—

Ca-shish, ca-shish.

"Tickets, please!"

Clippety-clip.

"Close all the windows!"

Spitter-spat-spit.

Past lighted houses—
Clackety-clack.

Out of the city—
Shackety-shack.

Gathering speed—
A ratter-tat-tat.

Into the black—
A clatter-clat-clat.

The ting of the rain—
Ping-itta-pang.

The ding of the crossings—
Cling-itta-clang.

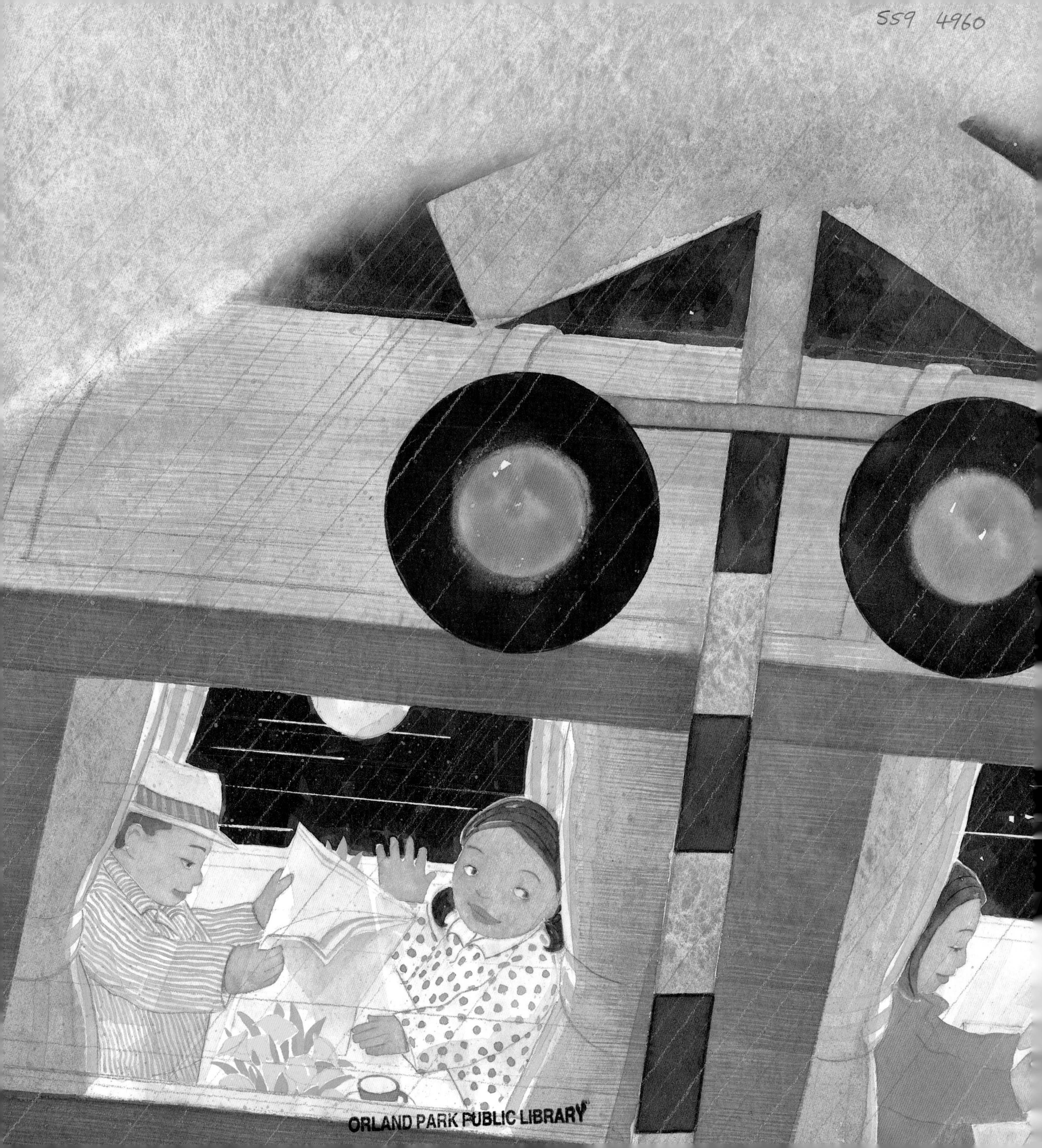

Over the bridge—

Whooshety-wish.

Racing the moon—

Swishety-swish.

Whistle past rivers,
Whoosh through the tunnels,
Roar down the plains.

And all of the time,
Always the same. . . .

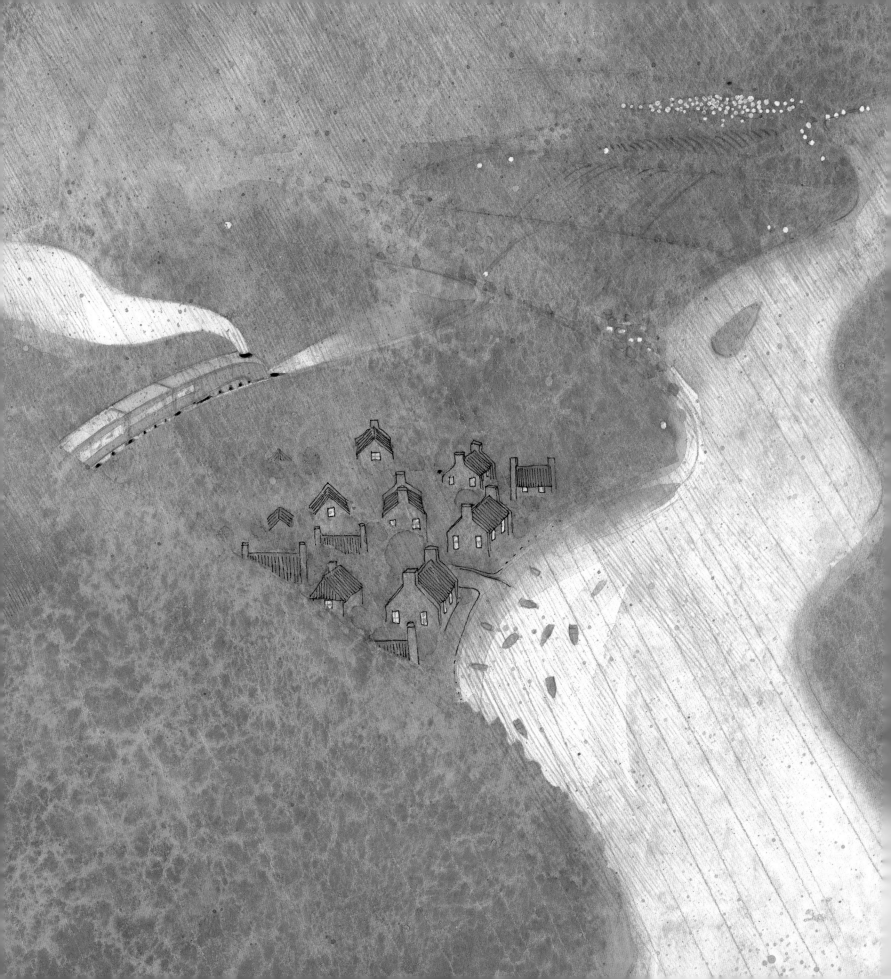

The wail of the wind, the sway of the train,
The strum of the wheels to the beat of the rain—
A pitter-pat-pat, a pitter-pat-pat,
A pittery-pittery-pittery-pat.

Storm past the stations; no one alights.

Safe in my sleeper, I steam through the night.

Ssshhhhhhhhhhhhhhhhh,
Ssshhhhhhhhhhhhhhhh,
Ssshhhhhhhhh.